To the Abbasi family
thankyou for your support

Aut Swim

Magic Mangroves

AXEL SAINZ

Chapter One

———❧———

"Hey, Joan, guess what I just found out," exclaimed Keith, my friend since kindergarten. When we were kids, we both pretty much acted the same, but the older we grew, the more we began to drift. Now that we're in college, we're completely different.

"What? What did you just find out, Keith?" I asked sarcastically, knowing it was probably something completely ridiculous, which I was about to be proven right.

He continued, "Calm down, will you? Look, I know I may not always be the most reliable person in the world when it comes to facts, but hear me out this time. So I found this place that apparently is nowhere to be found on any maps, and there are no records of it anywhere—"

"Okay, but how am I supposed to believe that you, someone who looks at their phone in class all day, found an area completely hidden from all other forms of exploration? Man, you barely get out of your dorm! And come to think of it, you probably got this from some rando on the internet, scrolling through your phone in class, didn't you?"

"Maybe. Shut up. So, as I was saying, before I was so rudely interrupted, I was scrolling through the zoom-in parts of random online maps, which may or may not have happened in class, and apparently the guy taking pictures of the place got lazy or something, cuz he didn't even bother to put them into the map! What sucked, though, was that it was so foggy that all I could see was a busted-up sign that said 'Magic Mangroves.' When I went to look the place up to get to know a little more about it, I got absolutely

1

nothing, so now all I know about the place is its location and that it has a big ol' sign with 'Magic Mangroves' written on it near what I'm guessing is the entrance," he explained.

I rubbed my forehead in frustration. "And why in the name of anything that ever existed would I believe that?" I asked.

Keith stopped to think about what he had just explained to me for a minute or so. Finally, he threw up his hands and yelled, "You know what? Fine! Fine! Don't believe me! I'll let you do your research, and when you decide to be a millionaire, come talk to me!" He spun away from me and walked out of the hall.

Later that day, when my classes were all over, I went back to my dorm and went straight to my laptop to research Magic Mangroves.

It was almost midnight when my roommate, Ed, finally came back from his classes and grocery shopping. He sat the groceries down on the table, plopped on his bed, and asked, "Studying again? Didn't you just have a test, like, last week?"

"Yes, I did," I replied. "But I'm not studying. I'm trying to research something."

He sat up to look at what I was looking up, and with a confused look on his face asked, "Magic Mangroves? What? Are you just trying to come up with some good alliterations or something? Because if you are, I've been looking for a use for the term *crazy chameleon* since I was, like, twelve or something."

I turned around in my swivel chair. Rubbing my forehead, I attempted to explain. "No, it's just that Keith was telling me about this place he found on the zoom-in part of an internet map that wasn't actually listed on the map and had no online records, but I said it probably wasn't real. To prove myself right, I started to research it, but then I realized that whether or not what he says is true, there would be no online record of it, and now I'm just frustrated."

Ed just nodded, pretending to understand, and asked, "Well, did he send you the link to wherever he found what he's claiming to have found?"

"Actually," I exclaimed, "he did!" I went to the email of my laptop and clicked on the link he sent me. When I clicked on it, it sent me to an area of an online map that only showed an island in the middle of the Atlantic Ocean. I zoomed in on the island until the screen was almost entirely white with fog, revealing only the silhouettes of nearby trees, with one exception. Directly by the camera, which was the only thing that was fully visible, was a very chipped and moldy wooden sign that read "Magic Mangroves." I couldn't even zoom in on any other part of the island, just that part. That was all I could see. Ed and I looked at each other and back at the screen.

Ed laid back down with his hands on his head and just murmured, "Weird ..."

Not much later, Ed went to bed, but I stayed up to research more. I tried looking up so many things, and the only thing that came up with results was "map of Atlantic Ocean," which didn't even show that the island existed.

When I finally decided to give up, I looked at the time, and it was three o'clock in the morning. My classes started at seven o'clock, so I went to bed as quickly as possible. But I couldn't sleep. I couldn't stop thinking about the Magic Mangroves.

CHAPTER TWO

———— ❧ ————

W hen I woke up the next morning, I immediately began to panic. Ed wasn't there, and our classes started at the same time. I got up and prepared for my classes as quickly as I could. As I ran to my first class, the whole time I was thinking, *Please don't be late.*

I burst through the door of my classroom, and the lesson had already started. As I quietly walked to my seat, my entire class stared at me with a look of shock on their faces. They were surprised that I, of all people, showed up late to class. Well, that is, all but one person, had a look of shock on their face. Keith sat in his chair, silently and desperately trying to hold in laughter. He stared right at me as I glared at him.

The rest of the day went as normal. Keith mocked me for staying up all night and showing up late to class.

When all my classes ended that day, I went straight to the library, as the internet had proven to be useless on the topic. I looked all over for any, and I mean any, book related to the topic.

I gave up on the library and dejectedly walked over to my dorm to hopefully go to bed early and get at least a little more energy. But when I got to my bed, I couldn't sleep. I kept thinking about the Magic Mangroves. Finally, I decided to try searching one more thing before I giving up. I got up, went over to my desk, and turned on my laptop. I went to the internet and typed in "News reports on magic usage." Of course, there were many reports of crazy people claiming to have seen or used magic and the news reporters making a commotion of it. As I scrolled down, I began seeing more and more reports of fishermen going missing, seemingly all near the same area—the same area in which Keith found the Magic Mangroves. Not only that but an even stranger recurrence began to reveal itself to me. The birds stopped midair, appearing to make a ripple in the sky where they stopped as if hitting a somewhat weak wall of some kind, yet there was seemingly nothing in front of them. The same occurrence seemed to happen with planes, but because they don't fly as low as birds, they just sort of bounced off the top of the invisible barrier.

The next morning, since I actually got a sufficient amount of sleep, I got up early and began planning for a trip to the Magic Mangroves. My college was definitely on the more forgiving side of granting time off. We were nearing spring break, so this was the perfect time for a trip. I found a dock in Florida online that could conveniently take me pretty much anywhere. Once I had finished planning the trip, all I needed to do was pay for my ticket. While I thought about how many tickets I wanted, I realized that of all people, Keith would want to visit the Magic Mangroves more than anyone. All I was worried about was the fact he might not want to go with me—namely because I yelled at him for believing in what he saw and then went online and began researching it without telling him.

After our classes ended, I confronted him. "Keith, look, I know what I said about you and the Magic Mangroves, but—"

"Are you about to ask if I want to go with you, my best friend since kindergarten, to a place we have little to no information on, which I recently discovered," he interrupted, shutting my lips with his index finger and thumb.

I nodded, and he looked at me with an expression that I could only describe as saying, "Did you really think I would say no?"

I managed to get the words through my lips despite him holding them closed. "So is that a yes?"

He nodded and explained that he would pay me however much his ticket cost.

Despite the fact I thought it would be, it wasn't even close to being the most heart-wrenching part of the planning.

After running out to get supplies for the trip, as I assumed the Magic Mangroves were completely unexplored and knew we would be there for most of the break, I returned to my dorm to see Ed lying on his bed, all of the lights off, on his laptop.

6

Ever since we became roommates, Ed and I had been growing closer and closer. By this point, since Ed was slightly older and more mature than me, he'd become an older brother figure to me. He had gotten me through hard times, helped me with projects, and I had done the same for him. We had shared a lot with each other.

So much so, that he probably knows slightly less, if not as much about me as Keith does. I know things about him that he would never share with anyone else, and because I respect him so much, I will not go into detail. Every day, when I return, he greets me as soon as I walk through the door. Today, however, even when greeted him, he said nothing.

"Hey, what's wrong, Ed? Something got you upset? Do you wanna talk about it," I asked, beginning to worry.

"I looked at your laptop," he said. "Why didn't you tell me you were going to the middle of the Atlantic Ocean? Do you understand how dangerous that is? Do you understand how worried I was about you when you wouldn't answer your phone?" He turned on his phone, and showed it to me. It was open to my contact on his messaging app. It showed a series of messages, each seeming more frantic than the last. I looked at his face, and his eyes seemed to be tearing up, I assume due to stress.

"I'm so sorry, I completely forgot to tell you about it. C'mon Ed, you know I don't keep secrets from you! I promise, I was going to tell you," I stammered, desperately trying to come up with an explanation to ease his nerves. I felt awful. Although I didn't realize it, another reason Ed felt like a big brother to me, besides the things I already explained, was that he cared about me. He would always ask me where I was going before I went anywhere. If I was going somewhere, or with someone unfamiliar, he would always offer to take me there. Although it had never occured to me, he did that because he cared. He worried about me, and didn't want me to get hurt. He always encouraged me to be the best me I could be.

"All I want to let you know is - whatever you need, I'll help. Funds, supplies, anything, just tell me. I don't approve of it, and don't think it would be safe, but if it makes you happy, I'll help. I can tell from the amount of time you've spent researching this, that you're really passionate about it, whatever it is. Plus, I'm not your mom, I can't tell you what to do," he explained, laughing as he said the last part, wiping a tear from his face.

Chapter Three

T wo weeks had passed, and spring break had arrived. I explained to my parents and older sister what I would be doing, but I didn't want to worry them too much, so all I said was that I would be going out of the country for the duration of the break with Keith.

Keith and I decided that the boat tickets plus plane tickets would be too expensive, so we would drive halfway across the country, from where we were in Minnesota, all the way to Florida. As one could tell, we weren't exactly the best decision-makers back then.

We left on the first day of Spring Break at around nine o'clock at night, as I thought it would be best if Keith would be asleep during the drive, so that he wouldn't be showing me a post on social media every five minutes. We agreed that I would be doing most of the driving, as I can drive without road-rage, and an hour through the drive, I already begin regretting that decision. It was dark outside, as one would expect it to be at ten o'clock at night, and despite the fact that there were other cars driving around and all of the streetlights were on, I still felt dangerously alone without Keith being awake, and, as an extrovert, feeling alone wasn't the best thing for me. At this time, I began wondering how my dad, who was also an extrovert, and who was also the one doing most of the driving out of my parents, would do the road trips that we would so often do as a family, when I was younger. I suppose it was just that he had everything planned out when we did those road trips. That, and he most likely got used to the feeling of my mom being asleep next to him, in the passenger seat, occasionally waking up to check on him, and ask if he wanted her to drive for a little bit, to which, the answer was always no, and the sound of me and my sister snoring in the back seats, with my unconscious body desperately fighting the seatbelt, as I was always moving when I slept, and my sister occasionally waking up, which, thinking back on it, she probably got from my mom, and readjusting me.

After some time of me thinking of my childhood, and the things my parents would do for each other, and for the family, I realized the sun was rising, and checked the time. It was six o'clock in the morning. I decided that it would probably be best if we spent the nights leading up to the arrival to our destination in a bed-and-breakfast, and used the daytime to drive. I woke up Keith to ask if that would be a good idea, or if we should just keep driving, taking occasional breaks.

He answered, half-asleep, "Yeah, I actually felt bad once I realized that you would be driving until the morning. Then I fell asleep. It probably would be best if we slept in a motel, or something of the sorts for a little bit, so you can rest." We did exactly that.

When I woke up, which was during the nighttime, we had to get back on the road, and I agreed to do the driving again, for some reason. However, instead of my childhood, the only thing on my mind this time around was the sudden change in weather, from clear skies to rainy. Then I saw it. The sign on the side of the road, saying, "Welcome to Kentucky!" For the rest of the ride, or at least, until our next break, all I thought about was the fact that we were halfway there.

Chapter Four

I somehow pulled through, and made it all the way to Florida, having taken only one break to sleep. However, I was extremely tired, so I decided to leave my car in a trustworthy place, (an unknown grocery store parking lot) and take the nearest bus down to the docks we needed to be at.

The point of taking the bus was sort of taken away because of how pretty the ocean is in Florida. I couldn't sleep for most of the ride, because I was just staring at the ocean the whole time.

Before I knew it, we were already at the docks. Apparently, Keith and I were either extremely tired, or completely forgot that we had a deadline for this project of ours, because we got heavily sidetracked. There were several carts selling things that I would never even think of, such as sprinkle-coated hot sauce ice cream. It was also incredibly hot, and instead of just buying something to cool us down, Keith and I stopped at almost every store in between us and the dock we need to be at.

When we finally realized that we should have been doing things quicker and more efficiently, and actually got to the dock we needed, it had a very confusing way of handling things. Essentially, it was a very small motor boat that could only fit up to three people, besides the man driving, and instead of even telling the man where you wanted to go, you had to either bring a map with the directions already clearly drawn, or be willing to give him directions for the whole ride. I brought my own map with the directions written out on it, so, needless to say, the ride was quiet.

In order to be interesting to my readers, since not much actually happened on the ride itself, I might as well explain what I saw. I first noticed that the water was somehow blue, and crystal-clear at the same time. It's hard to explain how, or even what it looked like, but the water was simply beautiful. The boat had wooden seats, and was completely white, besides a blue stripe, wrapping around the entire boat. Because of how much sleep he got, Keith was very energetic the whole ride, pointing out every little thing he noticed, and elaborating on what it reminded him of. The man driving the boat had a full, brown beard and mustache, a shirt stained with, what I hope is ketchup, and cargo shorts. His eyes were covered by a blue beach hat. He barely talked.

I could tell the driver was getting suspicious, when the part of the map that I identified as our destination neared, on the map, yet when he looked around, there was nothing to be seen. However, I did notice that, somehow, there was a specific area that caused my vision to get blurry when I looked at it, nearing us.

Suddenly, I felt a very harsh throbbing in my head, and when I looked at Keith, his breathing seemed very sharp and panicked, yet I couldn't hear him. I looked over at the driver of the boat, and, as his eyes rolled back, he collapsed onto the floor of the boat. Then everything went dark, and I was able to hear Keith crying for a very brief moment before I passed out.

CHAPTER FIVE

———⚬✦⚬———

When I awoke, Keith and the boat driver were nowhere to be found. "Keith? Keith! Keith, where are you," I yelled into the distance. I began to panic. I had no clue where I was, what direction I came from, or where the people I came with were. All I knew was that I was stranded on an island with a presumably dangerous rainforest ahead.

Then I realized something. The backpacks Keith and I took on the trip, full of water, food, and mapping were washed ashore, next to planks and shreds of white and blue wood, from what I assume is the boat.

I pushed my arms through the loops of both backpacks, one arm in the loop of one backpack, the other in the loop of the other backpack, and headed off into the rainforest ahead of me.

Immediately upon entering the rainforest, the climate around me completely changed from hot and clear, to warm and humid. I'm not entirely sure how, but despite the air being completely clear besides the humidity, I could make out the sound of crackling fire. I foolishly assumed the best.

I yelled out into the rainforest, "Keith, is that you? What are you doing out here?"

As I continued walking, the sky became clouded with grey, and the air smelled of burning, yet it still wasn't hot. I continued walking still. There was a large cluster of vines blocking me, so I pushed through them, and on the other side was a sign. "Magic Mangroves," it read. I looked behind me, and the cluster of vines had become a stone wall that stretches for miles. From the sign, there was a path leading to my left, a path leading to my right, and a swamp ahead of me, with a wooden bridge stretching far enough to be hidden by the smoke, leaving me with a decision to make.

I decided to turn left. The path to the left was made of rocks, and as I walked, the smell of smoke got stronger. Most of the path had been right next to the stone wall, and it began to slowly drift away from the wall, as I continued, and eventually I was in a village of stone houses, each with a chimney, with smoke pouring out from it. Each house had a lit torch on either side of the door. Somehow, each torch emitted a different color.

As I continued further into the village, I heard a voice. It was singing. I froze. Considering what had happened and what I had seen, I had no clue what it could have possibly been coming from. There had been small stone walls along the path of this village, about three feet tall, so I decided to hide behind one. I quietly looked over the wall, and a dark figure was cheerfully walking in my direction. That was where the singing was coming from. My breathing got heavier and heavier. I went back down to hide. My heart stopped as I heard a gasp, followed by the sound of footsteps stopping. I looked over the wall again, and my eyes were met with the eyes of a woman in a red cloak. She had brown hair, very welcoming eyes, and a jovial smile, full of pure happiness. Hoping she didn't see me, I hid again behind the wall.

"Hello? You don't need to hide from me, friend. I won't hurt you," the woman called out. I knew she was talking to me. I slowly came out from behind the wall.

"My name is Joan, and I'm looking for my friend. He's around 4'9." Brown hair. Have you see him," I asked.

"I'm sorry, no, I haven't," she replied, looking at me. "Jeez, you're really sunburnt. And you've got more cuts on you than I can count! Come to my home, I'll heal you up," she told me, gesturing for me to follow.

I looked down, and my upper knee was split, I was bleeding from my arm, and my entire body was reddish-pink and covered in cuts. It's amazing how much adrenaline can cover up in one's head. I followed her.

She took me through the village, and as far as I could tell, every house was the same. Stone cottages, each with a chimney, with smoke pouring from it.

We got to her home, and, although I'm still not sure what I was expecting, I was disappointed with the fact that her home looked exactly like the others. She opened the wooden door, and inside was an open and violently burning furnace. What confused me then, but makes sense now, is the fact that the floor and ceiling were wooden, yet there weren't any burn marks so to speak. The woman pulled out a wooden chair from a stone table and gestured me to sit. When I sit down, she walks into a seperate room, giving me time to process what had happened to me. I began thinking of my family. They have no clue what I'm going through right now, or even where I am for that matter. I thought of Ed. He just started trusting me with projects like this, and now I might be stuck here forever.

As I thought, I realized that pain began spreading through my body, starting with my knee. At first, all I felt was a sting, which evolved into a burning soreness, and a very raw and burning sensation all over my body. The longer I thought about the pain, however, the worse it hurt.

Just as I was contemplating giving up and passing out, the woman ran out of the room, arms absolutely full of different sized and colored bottles, which she drops on the table in front of me.

"Okay, how did you get hurt? Well, besides the burning, that is," she asked, opening a bottled labeled "For burns on non-fire users."

"Well, I don't remember a whole lot prior to being here," I responded. "Would it help to tell you that I came from the same side of the island that the 'Magic Mangroves' sign is facing?"

She scratched her head, and muttered, "I mean, I guess … it does tell me what didn't hurt you, though." With that said, she selected several different bottles, each with very different labels.

She instructed me to lay flat on my stomach on the bed that was in the same room as us, and I did as I was told. I suppose, although needless to say at this point, it's important to address the fact that this whole time, my shirt was at the shore at which I washed up, in shreds.

She opened the bottle that was labeled "For burns on non-fire users" and began carefully tilting it over my body.

She stopped tilting it, and laughed, "Where are my manners? My name is Umi, nice to meet you."

Confusedly, I asked, "Isn't that an Egyptian name? I don't know where we are, but I know we're not in Egypt."

"Well, yes, it is an Egyptian name, but in the Magic Mangroves, there are a variety of origins from which people come," she informed me.

I began, "Oh, well that's pretty interesting - ouch!" I was interrupted by the burning sensation of a strange liquid being poured all over my back. I reached to wipe it off, and Umi smacked my hand.

"Don't wipe it, it needs to be absorbed into your skin first, so it can heal your burns. For now, if you can handle even more pain, you can rub this into the wound on your knee," she firmly instructed, handing me a bottle labeled with "For cuts/poisoning."

After what felt like hours of excruciating pain, I was instructed by Umi to rest on the bed. Both of us were confused at the time, so we both resorted to asking questions.

She asked, "So what do you use, that you're so hurt, friend?"

I felt as if I misheard her. I asked, "Pardon?"

"What part of the Magic Mangroves are you from," she restated.

I figured it was just how the people there asked each other where they're from. "Oh, I'm not from the Magic Mangroves," I replied. After that statement, her facial expression instantly went from jovial and welcoming to confused and mildly frightened.

She very seriously asked, "How did you get in here? Only magic users can get through the barrier. Well, magic users and.. Him … but you are not him, I can tell." Her question and statements brought me to the purest form of confusion.

"You must be kidding. Magic? I mean, I suppose that would make the name of this place make more sense, but there is no possible way that magic exists! I refuse to believe you," I stubbornly told Umi.

She opened her palm and muttered, "Small flare," and in her palm appeared a small flame that wasn't burning her, and seemed to just stay in place. I flinched out of shock. I had no words. "Now, tell me how you got here," she instructed.

After explaining how, once we got within a certain distance of the island, everyone on the boat blacked out and when I awoke, everyone was gone, Umi muttered to herself, "I'm guessing the blacking out was the effect of the barrier … but that makes it so even you don't know what you did."

"Well, now you've got some explaining to do, Umi. Explain this whole 'magic' thing to me. And the barrier. Explain what that's all about," I demanded.

Umi began, "Well, although you probably don't know this, due to you being a non-magic user, roughly a thousand years ago, magic was alive and well. Of course there were some people who were against magic, but almost everyone used it. There were thousands, maybe even millions of different kinds of magic. But eventually, as time went on, magic began slowly disappearing. People began to find other ways to get things done without magic. Eventually, there were only seven kinds of magic, used by very little people: my magic, and the magic of this town, Fire Magic, Bio Magic, Lightning Magic, Metal Magic, Mind Magic, Ice Magic, and Dark Magic. People even started hating magic, calling it a crime against nature, so we magic users secluded ourselves on this island. The barrier exists to keep non-magic users from discovering the island, so of course I'm not sure what exactly it does, but I do know that it makes the island virtually invisible. Now, no non-magic users can get in or out of the island, but magic users can move freely in and out, just in case we need to get a taste of society. Oh, and everyone, no matter if they choose to use it or not, has a birth magic that disables them from learning any spells of other magics, but enables them to immediately learn spells from whatever magic their birth magic is, as long as they try. Does that explain everything?"

I swallowed hard and nodded, trying to let all the information sink in. Then I realized something. "Hey wait, does that mean I'm stuck here," I asked, my panic slowly rising.

"Well, I think so, yes. I do know, however, that the barrier was made using magic, and that the combined power of many types of magics could overpower that magic, so you may have a chance to get out of here," she attempted to reassure me. It didn't help. I tried to calm myself, realizing that panicking would get me nowhere.

"So where could my friend have gone? Is there any way to know he's safe," I asked.

"Well, there's no way he's in the middle of the Magic Mangroves, he would've been sent back by Him, so he could've gone to any of the five other villages. He could also be wandering around the island, but I doubt the Bio Magic users would allow that, they're very hospitable, and enjoy wandering around the island. And no, there is technically no way to know he is safe. He probably is, though, there's not a whole lot of deadly things around here," she explained.

"Hold on, you never explained who 'he' is. What's up with that," I half-asked, half-demanded.

She apologized, "Oh, yes, sorry. He is the ruler of this land. He is capable of giving and taking away life with the wave of a hand. He is all-powerful, shaped the land that we hide on to this day, protects us from the dangers of society, and has no known name."

"Ah, yes, I understand entirely," I said, absolutely not understanding. "So, if I were to look for my friend, where would I go first?"

"The Magic Mangroves consist of six different villages, as you know, that are all laid out in a circle, surrounding His headquarters, which is directly in the middle of the island. The mass of the villages and His headquarters is surrounded by a very thin area of rainforest. So, there are few places he could hide, or even be lost in. I suggest looking around the villages to see if anyone is taking care of him, first," Umi instructed.

Once I was done resting, and all of Umi's medicines had settled in, I could barely feel my burns and cuts. I decided that, since I was all healed up, I would be healthy and strong enough to continue on my own. As I was instructed, I set out for the villages first.

I picked up my backpack, walked out of the house, and began following a stone path, very similar to the one that brought me to the Fire Village. Suddenly, something hit my back, and I turned around to see a bag at my feet.

I looked up to see Umi running at me, shouting, "Hey, you can't leave without me! I have the medicines you might need along the way! And I have fire at my disposal! You don't even know your way around the Magic Mangroves!" The first two things, I admit, I can blow off as irrelevant, but the last thing was pretty important at the time. Plus, I think at this point I just really didn't want to go alone.

"Fine, you can come along. But just know, there's no promises that you'll come back alive," I joked. Then, we were on our way. "So. Which way am I headed, exactly?"

"On the path you're on right now, you're heading towards the bio village. Like I said, the Bio Magic users are very friendly, so you should be okay," she said.

It was about an hour into the walk to the Bio Village that I looked down and realized that this whole time, I wasn't wearing any shoes, and my feet were beginning to hurt. I also noticed that the smoke was clearing, the more we progressed. I suppose the smoke was coming from the Fire Village, after all. The clearing of smoke wasn't the only thing I noticed. The land around us was also becoming more and more lush, full of plants that I had never seen before in my life. Giant flowers, that opened and closed, rhythmically. Thick, thorny vines, that split into 5 directions at the ends. Glowing bead-like orbs at the ends off thin strings of vine, coming off of trees with twisting trunks. The sky, however, was still covered, but now with the leaves of trees above us, rather than smoke.

"So this is the Bio Village, huh," I asked. "Do all the villages look more like the Fire Village, or this?"

"Well, each village looks completely different from the others. That could either be a side-effect of the different magic users that inhabit them, or a precaution so that nobody gets lost," she told me.

From the trees, a giant multi-colored bird, with a long beak, multi-colored eyes, and three long feathers coming from the head dropped down, and screeched at us.

Panicked, I yelled, "I thought you said there weren't many deadly things here!"

Contrasting my panic, Umi very calmly said, "That's because it's not deadly." Again, she opened her palm, but this time, she muttered, "Flare," and a much larger flame appeared in her hand, behaving the exact same as the small flare, staying in place, not spreading, and not burning anything. "Sure, they don't like people very much, but they're frightened by bright light. I'm sure you could just wave your arms around and yell loudly, and they'd be scared off."

From this point on in the walk, I kept hearing the pitter-patter of frightened footsteps, and the curious cooing of birds above.

Finally, we came to a curtain of vines, which Umi pushed aside to reveal rows and rows of enormous trees, each with a completely wooden house on top, with a yellow glow coming from it. Umi leaned over and muttered to me, "Here we are. The Bio Village."

CHAPTER SIX

———— ❧ ————

U mi walked into the village, took a deep breath, and opened her arms towards it, as if welcoming it. "The Bio Village is such a refreshing change from the smoky, lifeless Fire village, wouldn't you agree," she asked me.

"I mean, I guess, but I haven't seen much of the Fire village yet, so I can't really say anything bad about it," I replied.

"Well I've lived in it, and I can tell you, although I am immune to burns or side-effects of smoke, the intense amount of smoke does get overwhelming," Umi said, seeming slightly annoyed.

Similarly to the giant bird, a young girl came down from the trees above, wearing clothes of leaves, and a holster, attached to her waist and short, bright red hair, which she wore in pigtails. She reached for the holster and pulled out a dagger, made from some kind of large animal fang and a thick branch, cut to make a handle, with a vine tying the tooth and branch together.

"State your name and purpose, intruders," the girl demanded. She looked at Umi and noticed the signs of her Fire Magic usage. She grinned, put away her makeshift dagger, and laughed, "Ha ha, just kidding! Just tell me what you guys need, and I can take you to it!" Nervously, I look at Umi for reassurance.

"Well, we're looking for someone. He's five feet, nine inches tall, brown-haired, and … what else, Joan," Umi asked. With both details she gave, she looked at me for approval.

"His name is Keith, and he never stops talking, have you seen him," I demanded.

"Um, no, but if he was here, I think the village elder would know," the girl said. The girl then turned around and walked off, motioning us to follow, so we did. The girl walked us through her village, holding a stick she found in front of her, jumping on the protruding tree roots and puddles, swinging the stick at bugs that flew near her.

"So, what's your name, small friend," Umi asked, to break the silence.

The girl looked at her, as if she was dozing off, and Umi woke her, and responded, "Oh, my name? I'm called Ber around here. Means 'bear'. Scary, huh?" She then turned around, obviously happy to have shared what her name means with us, and stopped, letting her arms hang in disappointment. "Oh," she said, "we're here."

In front of us was a tree, with the same twisting trunk all the other trees had, but it was extremely thick at the bottom, and got thinner and thinner, towards the top, until there was a fine tip at the top, where the tree exploded outwards into leaves. This tree was also much shorter than any of the other trees, and had a multi-colored trunk and deep blue leaves. At the front of the tree was a door and two windows, as well.

"C'mon, let's go inside," Ber yelled, excitedly. "You know, I've never actually met the elder. I mean, sure, I've heard all the stories about how he single-handedly made the Bio Village, but so has every other person in the village," she said, turning around to face us, and continued, walking backwards. "But now I get to meet him!" She opened the door and walked in, with us following close behind.

Inside was a very open room, with only a circle of mats on the floor, a very large, plump man on the sitting mat furthest from us, and a ham sandwich next to him.

Without opening his eyes, the man said, "Come, sit." Ber lit up with excitement, and ran to the mat next to the man. Umi and I followed, hesitantly.

Sitting on the mat on the other side of the man, I asked, "So, how did you know we were here? I mean, it seems like you didn't even open your eyes."

"I have many ways of doing the things I do," the man replied. "Now allow me to ask you a question. What do you wish to ask of me?"

22

Confused to how he knew we wanted to ask him a question, I told him, "Well, I was wondering if my friend was in this village. Would you know that?"

The man chuckled and replied, "Of course I would. Allow me to search for him for a moment." He went silent for a moment, as he looked upward, Umi and I looked around, confusedly, and Ber beamed, staring at the man, in awe.

He looked back down towards us and said, apologetically, "I'm very sorry, he doesn't appear to be here. At least, not now. Is that all?" I told him yes, and he said, "Well, I hope you find him. Happy travels, friend!"

As we were about to walk out the door, I realized that he didn't even know what Keith looked like, and as I was about to ask him how he knew he wasn't here without knowing what he looked like, and he just smiled and said, "I can tell when someone does not use magic." Horrified, I was about to beg him to not tell anyone, afraid I'd be hated, and he laughed, "Don't worry, your secret is safe with me!" The whole time, Ber looked at him, dazed, luckily not seeming to tell what he's saying. He looked over and saw her staring, and waved his hand at her towards us, and she snapped out of it, and skipped towards us, and out the door. We followed behind.

"Hey, did you see him? He was so big, and lively! You could definitely tell he knew his stuff. I mean, he was just so ... wise," Ber gushed on.

Umi looked over at me, then back at Ber, and said, awkwardly, "Well Ber, sorry to tell you, but we have to leave now. You know, we do still have a friend to look for-"

"Wait, what? Where are you guys going after this," she asked.

Umi tried explaining, "Well, on the path we're going, we'll end up in Lightning Village. Hopefully he'll be there-"

"Woah, you guys are going to Lightning Village? I hear that place is awesome! I'd love to go there sometime! I've always wanted to get out of here," Ber interrupted, once again. "Can ... can I come along?"

Umi kneeled down, put her hand on her shoulder, and said, comfortingly, "No, sorry, small friend. It might be dangerous. It will most definitely be long and strenuous, if we don't find our friend. Besides, your family would probably worry about you, and you wouldn't want to do that to them, would you?"

Ber replied, as if it were an obvious fact, "My family died a while ago. And before you worry about me, I'm a Bio Magic user, so I can make my own crops instantly. Plus, there's all kinds of animals in the Bio Village, so I just kind of hang out with them."

Umi arose, surprised, and said, "Oh. Well, I suppose it would be safer for you to come with us then, after all-"

Ber interrupted, this time with extreme enthusiasm, "Yes! Thank you, thank you, thank you, thank you! You will not regret this, I promise! I bet you won't even know I'm here!"

"Well, I suppose we'll be on our way then. There's nothing you'd like to do before we leave, right Joan? And you, Ber, there's nothing more you'd like to do or take with us before we leave," Umi checked. Both Ber and I said no, and just like that, we were once again on our way.

Chapter Seven

———— ⚬⎯⚬ ————

Ber led us to to the other side of the village, where Umi then took the lead, so that she may defend us from any possible dangers, as I didn't use magic, and Ber was just a child. We were on a similar stone path that led us to the Bio Village. Also similar to the path we came here on, it was full of lush, luxurious plants, and trees overhead. However, as we continued, the amount of plants began decreasing, and the sounds of wildlife were no more. Instead, somehow, I was hearing sounds of electronic music, and high-energy advertisements. It suddenly felt like I was back in the city. The stones in the path became tattered, stained, and lifted metal tiles. As we moved along, they become more straightened, and colorful. I looked ahead, and saw that the tiles ahead of us were flashing green, pink, yellow, and blue. I looked over at Umi and Ber, with Umi looking concentrated, and confused, and Ber looking amazed, and in disbelief.

We came to a giant, metal wall, with two automatic doors right next to each other. Umi looked at them, confusedly, and held back me and Ber, expecting them to be a trap, as they had no handles. I pushed her arm down, motioning for her to let her guard down, as I walked up to the doors and let them open on their own, and Umi looked terrified, while Ber excitedly ran up to them, wildly waving her arms, trying to close them back up. I walked through them, and motioned for Umi and Ber to follow. Despite how cocky I might have seemed, I, myself, was very confused on how this city existed, or why. Reluctantly, Umi followed. Ber was already through them, however, pulling my arm, trying to get me to continue.

Umi looked up, and for the first time, I saw Umi in awe, absolutely stunned with her surroundings. I was, at the time, expecting it to be a regular city, but when I turned and looked around, I saw high buildings, bright, colorful lights, busy streets, and people everywhere. It seemed every building had a giant screen on it, displaying an advertisement for its own company, or for a sponsor. As you can tell, I understood completely, but Umi, who was holding Ber's hand, as to not lose her in the crowd, was baffled, while Ber tried touching everything we passed. It was clear their personalities truly shined bright in this village.

Hours later, we had eaten, which was my chance to show Ber and Umi some of my favorite city foods, bought Ber and Umi pointless souvenirs, and had been walking around aimlessly, trying to come up with an idea for where Keith could possibly be. Finally, I spotted, through the crowd, a club advertising "Free arcade token with every drink," and I immediately knew where he would be. I started running toward it, motioning for Umi and Ber to follow. Once I got to the building, I looked behind me, and saw Umi carrying an ecstatic Ber, and realized that maybe I should've probably waited for Umi and Ber, as Ber probably couldn't run very fast. I then also realized that the bouncer probably wouldn't let us in with a child, and we were definitely not going to leave Ber outside, dagger and magic or not. Then, miraculously, a drunken man came stumbling out of the entrance, obviously forgetting that there was an exit, and the guard had to stop him, so we, using that time, got through.

Horrified at the amount of drunks, alcohol, and romance that was in the club, Umi reached for Ber and covered her eyes, holding her close. She motioned me to move along, while she left with Ber, and mouthed that she'll meet me outside. Once she left, I looked around and saw a sign that read "Arcade" and pushed through the sea of drunks and couples to get to it. In the arcade, it was even louder, full of people getting angry at video games, "controller issues," and each other. I walked around, looking for Keith, and finally, I spotted him at one of the machines, with around thirty plastic cups labeled "Water" around him, on the floor.

I tapped his shoulder, and, without looking away from his game, furiously tapping buttons, he said, "Look, I already told you, I'm gonna be here for a while. Sorry, buddy, I'm just too good!" He glanced over at me for a moment, then back at his game, then stopped completely to stare at me.

"Joan? Dude! Where were you? I've been looking for you everywhere … in this arcade …"

"What do you mean, 'where was I'? You left me at the boat! I'm the one who's been looking for you," I yelled at him, slightly frustrated. "In fact, how about you explain yourself outside, hm?"

He looked back over at his game, and complained, "Aw, but I've been doing so well-" Before he could finish his sentence, he looked back over at me, and saw my piercing glare. He reluctantly agreed, and followed me to the exit, where we met up with Umi and Ber.

"Keith, this is Umi and Ber. Ber, Umi, this is Keith. Also known as the traitor, who left me to die," I said.

Keith begged, "Oh come on Joan, you know I wouldn't do that to you! Please, hear me out!"

"Yeah, that's kind of why we're out here. Get to explaining, before I stop listening," I demanded.

"Okay, okay, so it started when I woke up, saw you scraped, burnt, and thin, and realized I was hungry, too. So, I ran through the rainforest, because I'm not the best at handling hunger, fell into the swamp, and saw some lights up ahead, so I assumed it was a city, which I was right about, and swam to it, hoping to find some food. There, happy," he asked at the end of his explanation.

Umi piped up and corrected him, "Well, actually you weren't right on assuming it was a city, as it is still technically a village, but whatever."

Keith, annoyedly told her, "Look, I'm not looking for corrections, I'm looking for forgiveness. But also, if you maybe want to give me your number later, I'll take it."

"Keith, she doesn't know what you mean. And even if she did, stop flirting with her, she's our guide and friend! I'll forgive you for now, but just know that you are on thin ice," I told him. He held out his arms for a hug, and I just held out my hand. It did nothing. He pulled me in for a powerful bear hug, and Ber joined in too, trying not to be left out. Keith reached out to pull in Umi, too, and she burned his hand, ending the hug immediately.

"Well, I guess we could leave the island now then, huh, Joan," he asked.

"How," I asked. "How could we possibly leave right now, Keith? We don't have a boat. We don't know where we are. And, you may not know

27

this one, but we need a combination of many different magics to escape the barrier that's trapping us here, and in case you haven't noticed, we have two." He just looked down at the ground, thinking.

He looked back up, first at Ber, then at Umi, and his frown curled into a grin, as he said, "I have an idea."

As we were about to sneak back into the club, to execute Keith's plan, Ber gasped, "Wait, you guys don't use magic? That's so lame! Oh man, wait 'till Becky the beaver hears about thi-"

Umi interrupted her, more serious than I had, and have seen her, "Ber, don't tell anyone about this, or else people might get hurt, including Keith, Joan, you, and I. Got it?" Ber silently nodded, and we continued.

When we got back to the entrance, the guard had returned, and we couldn't get back in. Then, Keith got another idea.

"Hey Ber," he kneeled down and said, "did you know that there was a trapped bird in there?"

Ber looked terrified, and asked, "What?"

"Yeah, there's this cage in there, and I'm pretty sure it's got a bird - maybe two - in it. A shame, really," he looked away, pretending to be sad. Then, he looked back up, and told her, "Oh wait a minute, I bet you could sneak in there just fine, set them free, and get out of there, what, with your size and dagger you got there, in your holster. Oh, unless you don't want to, I mean, that bird could suffer a little longer-"

Halfway through Keith's last sentence, Ber had already dashed into the club, with the bouncer noticing, but too fast to get caught by him. The bouncer then ran into the club, attempting to retrieve the dashing Ber. I realized Keith's plan had worked.

"You are a manipulative man, Keith," I coldly scolded him.

Keith turned away, and said, "Oh, stop, you flatter me!"

Once the bouncer went back inside the building, we took our chance, and moved in. Umi, without anyone noticing, picked up Ber, and continued on behind us, with Ber screaming about the birds. Keith walked back into the arcade, and for a moment, I got the idea that he just wanted to play more video games, but discarded that idea, as the video game he was at was occupied, yet he continued on.

He took us to a two-player fighting game, that was being played by a very skinny, teenage boy, with acne, glasses, buck-teeth, a bowl-cut, and a hunched back, and a very large, muscular man, with a buzzcut and tattoos. I watched, horrified, as Keith tapped the large man on his shoulder, and the man's expression changed from confident, and joyous, to annoyed, and angry.

The man, without looking away from his game, attempted to shoo away Keith, "Look, kid, I'm kind of in the middle of something, here. Scram."

Keith, being his cocky self, told the man, "Oh no, not this time, Nick! You took my money, and cheated your way out of a bet using intimidation! And when I said 'You'll pay your end of the bet, and I'll make sure of it,' I was serious!"

The man, Nick, I assume, turned around and muttered the words, "Crackle," and electricity crackled in the palm of his hand, as a wicked smile stretched across his face. He then saw Umi, with her flare prepared, and Ber, with her dagger drawn. Needless to say, his crackle disappeared. He put his hands in the pockets of his jeans, and asked, annoyed, "Alright, kid, what do you want? Money? Here, take it, and leave me alone." He threw his money at Keith, and turned back towards his game.

Keith, happy that he scared Nick, said, "No, I don't want your money anymore, actually." Nick turned back towards us, confused. "We want you to come with us to let us leave this island. And, before you ask, no, we don't use magic, and therefore, do need the help of several different magic users, and if you tell anyone, we will hurt you. If you agree, however, and mess with us, we will also hurt you. Got it?"

Nick nodded, angrily, and pushed passed us, demanding, "Okay, if we're going, we're going now." We all gave each other a glance, shrugged, and followed behind Nick. Ironic, as he was the one who was supposed to be following us.

CHAPTER EIGHT

⎯⎯⎯◦⌇◦⎯⎯⎯

I suppose, now that I think about it, that it actually did make the most sense for Nick to lead us, before we lead him, as the Lightning Village is complicated, and full of turns and people, which he would know his way around. It's a shame that our guide had us on his sour side, though. It was also a shame that we had to keep stopping, because Ber was laughing at Keith and I for not using magic.

We came to what I assume is the other end of the village, which was very similar to the end we entered through, as it was just a blank, metal wall, with two automatic doors in the middle of it. I decided it was the other end, as, right when we walked through the doors, we felt a blast of cold air. We lost our guide, as Umi fell to the fetal position, and began shivering, unable to move, and Nick was forced to carry her, as he was the only one who could. It was up to me to guide us.

Immediately, I realized how much trouble we were in, as I had no clue where I was going, and the ground became much more barren, and coated in snow as we continued. The land ahead of us also became less and less visible, as cold, harsh wind picked up, carrying snow with it. It was at this point that the entire group began losing hope. Incredible, how easily the party had accepted death, despite this not being anywhere near the hardest part of our journey. At least, to me.

Then, as I too, almost gave up and submitted to the harsh environment, I saw a light in the distance.

"Help! Please! Over here," I yelled, hopelessly, into the distance, my voice breaking, and my body shivering. I saw the light stop moving, and

31

then move quickly towards us. I closed my eyes, hoping for closure on this part of the journey, not knowing whether or not I would wake. I felt a sudden warmth spread through me, then everything went black, and I was no longer conscious.

CHAPTER NINE

⸺◦∿◦⸺

When I awoke, I looked around. I was lying on a bed, covered in two thick, fur blankets, and I had a wool sweater on. I looked to my left, and saw Ber, sitting upright, also on a bed, dangling her legs off the side, wrapped in a blanket, sipping hot chocolate out of a mug. She lit up when she saw me awake, and aware.

"Joan! You're awake! How'd you sleep," she asked. Any other time, I would've been concerned as to why she was so okay with waking up in an unfamiliar place, but now, I was just confused.

"Um, good ... where did you get that mug," I asked Ber. I looked around more, and saw two more beds, Keith in one, and Umi in the other, both asleep, and covered in blankets. Nick was asleep on the floor, also covered in blankets, but neither blanket completely covered him.

Ber pointed at a door frame, and told me, "Oh, the nice lady who helped us did. She went back in there to make some for you guys."

I hadn't noticed until now, but this whole time, we had been in an igloo. Strange, how something made of ice could be so warm.

At the moment Ber told me where she got her hot chocolate from, a blonde-haired, blue-eyed woman wearing a thick blue winter jacket, winter boots, jeans, and mittens walked through the door frame, holding another mug. She looked at me, blowing on the hot chocolate.

"Oh," the woman said, "you're awake now. This was for me, but you can have it. You need it more than I do, after all." She nervously laughed. Something told me she wasn't very extroverted. I took the mug.

I sipped the hot chocolate, and exclaimed, "Hey, this is really good! Do you make these from scratch?"

Her face turned red, and she looked away, muttering, "Oh, thank you, yeah I do, but it's no big deal or anything, though. Wait, I actually have a question for you. What are you doing here, in the Ice Village, with no Ice Magic users, and a Fire, Bio, and Lightning magic user?"

"Oh, well, It's kind of a long story ... hey, wait a minute, how did you know what magic Umi, Ber, and Nick used," I asked.

The woman pulled up a wooden chair, which I guess I just hadn't noticed until now, and told me, "I can tell, based on what you guys are are wearing, what magic you use. Every village has a very unique fashion style. Also, I've got a lot of free time, don't worry."

"Well, it all started when Keith, the smaller boy, found this place, the Magic Mangroves, on an online map, and we decided to come here, and explore. What we didn't realize is that there was a magic barrier around it, that would destroy our boat, and that we wouldn't be able to leave here without being magic users, and would have to use a collection of different magics to break the barrier. So now we're walking around the Magic Mangroves, looking for people who will help Keith and I to break the barrier, and get out of here," I explained.

The woman's mouth stretched into a wide smile, and she told me, "I can come with you! Well, that is, if you want me to, I don't have to if you don't want me to, I just thought it'd be nice to get out of here for once-"

I cut her off, "No, please come with us, we'd really not like to wander through the Ice Village, looking for someone else to come with us. Honestly, I don't even know how you live here, this place is dangerous! But, I would like to know your name, that would kind of help us, you know."

Her face lit up, and I could tell she was struggling to contain her excitement, and she exclaimed, "Thank you so much! I'll never be able to repay you for this! Oh, by the way, my name is Dimma. I seriously cannot thank you enough!"

I introduced myself, and the three of us spent the next couple of hours playing card games, hide-and-go-seek, chess, and doing jigsaw puzzles, while we waited for the others to wake up. Of course, we pretended Ber won all of the games we played, while we discreetly decided whether Dimma or I won. Then, Nick woke up, and shortly after, so did Umi and Keith, simultaneously.

After everyone had their hot chocolate, Dimma, excitedly, asked me, "So, everyone's awake now, and had their hot chocolate. Does that mean we can leave now?" I looked at everyone, for confirmation, and once everyone nodded at me, I nodded at Dimma, and she jumped with excitement. "What are we waiting for then? Let's go," she exclaimed, running out the door. Immediately after, she came back inside, grabbed us all thick, fur jackets, including one for herself, and then walked back out the door. I noticed a pattern, with the people I was meeting. They usually don't want to wait to leave their homes. I suppose it makes sense, though, as every part of the Magic Mangroves is so different, so spending your whole life in one part of it must feel like you're being kept from something so much more than just "home."

CHAPTER TEN

---ᴄᴠᴏ---

U mi, Ber, Nick, Keith, and I all grabbed our jackets, and followed Dimma as quickly as possible, as to not lose our guide, especially here, where navigation is almost impossible. She stopped every now and again, so we could catch up. I found, and still find it strange that the busiest and most populated village of the Magic Mangroves would be placed right next to the most desolate and lonely part of the Magic Mangroves, as, there were barely any houses. It would make sense that there were barely any people in the Ice Village if they all acted like Dimma did, however.

There isn't much to explain about this part of the journey, so I'll just skip to the next part. I will explain, however, that the snow of the Ice Village seemed very powdery and soft, yet when I picked a handful of it up, it pricked my hands many times, as if it were shards of ice, rather than snow.

We arrived to the edge of the Ice Village, and the ground turned from snow to frozen-over metal, and ahead of us stood a steel wall, much like the Lightning Village, but it was taller, and neater, with a code-locked door, instead of an automatic sliding door. As we got closer, I could see that the code lock had nothing but a keypad, and what seemed to be a camera on it. I looked at the door stumped. We had no way of getting in.

Suddenly, the camera lens turned red, and a voice, coming from nowhere, as far as we could see, asked us, "What are you doing here? I can tell none of you are Metal Magic users, so you have no place here."

I stepped up and replied, "Oh, we're very sorry, but we've been trying to look for someone who could help my friend here and I get out of the Magic Mangroves. You see, uh, well … we're new here. Yeah, that's it! We're new to the Magic Mangroves, and new to using magic at all, and we'd like to go back home, but we don't know how yet. May we please come in?"

We heard a very obvious sigh, and then the door slid open, with a hiss. We walked inside, with Umi and Ber looking terrified, and amazed, and everyone else looking completely unphased.

When we walked in, we were inside of a giant castle-like building, with the walls, floor, and ceiling made of steel, lit by only torches. We were on a long, red carpet, leading up to a very tall, steel throne, with four guards, two on each side, each wearing a full suit of knight armor, and wielding a spear. On the throne, sat a a short, round man, wearing plates of gold all over his body, a gold crown, and many jeweled rings.

The man got down from his throne, and, walking towards us, said, "You know, I do apologize, but I also know not of how to leave the Magic Mangroves, so I may be of little help. I am the king of the Metal Village, and, although it is a small village, I can promise you that each and every one of the civilians I rule are excellent fighters, and will protect you every step of the way."

I smiled, and told him, "Well, thank you, that's very kind of you! Do you have any suggestions for who we should take with-"

"I never said I would just give you my subjects," he interrupted. "Unless … you have something to trade?"

I looked at everyone, and came to the conclusion that we had nothing. Then I remembered that I did have something, though it wasn't the best idea to trade.

"Well, I have this backpack full of food-," I hesitated.

The king interrupted, "Ooh, give it!" He reached out for it.

Yanking the backpack away from him, I scolded, "I never said I would trade it!"

"Well why not," he begged. "Do you not need a guardian to assist you on your journey? I can offer you my greatest guardian!"

"Hm, fine, I guess I'll budge," I pretended. He called over someone named "Damien." One of the guards, a taller one, marched towards us, but halfway toward us, he dropped his spear, and repeatedly tried, but failed at picking it back up, and he even dropped his helmet while picking his spear up, revealing a man with straight brown hair reaching his shoulders, a strong jawline, and shiny green eyes. He finally picked up his spear and helmet, and hurried over to us.

"I apologize greatly for this inconvenience, my lord," he said, not looking at any of us, even the king, with his chest puffed, and lip quivering.

The king reached up and smacked him on the side of his torso, as that was all he could reach, and yelled at him, "You imbecile! You've wasted our poor guests' time! Don't worry about disappointing me anymore, however, as you'll be assisting these six on their journey, got it?"

Damien, I'm assuming, looked very dejected, and begged, "My lord, I am so sorry, I swear it'll never happen again! Please, don't get rid of me just yet! I swear, I'll get better!" The king simply put up his hand, and turned his head the other way.

"Do not attempt to beg for pardon with me, Damien. Besides, your clumsiness is not the reason for me giving you away. It's actually because these kind people have offered me food, and in return, I must give them my most skilled fighter to assist them, and not even you can deny that you are the most skilled fighter of my subjects, no matter how clumsy you are," the king explained.

Damien blushed, and, shedding a tear, said, "Why thank you, my lord, I promise I will not disappoint! I will be the best guard for these folks that anyone has ever seen!"

The king attempted to pat Damien's shoulder, although he couldn't reach, so he just patted his arm, and demanded he lead us to the other end of the Village. Damien bowed, and marched off, gesturing for us to follow.

Damien led us through a village with stone houses, with straw roofs, and chimneys on top. The ground was dirt. The most notably "metal" things about the Metal Village was the king's castle, and a very large factory with smoke pouring from it, completely made of metal, on one of the ends of the village, although, due to the size of the village, I wasn't completely sure which end it was.

I turned to Umi, and, to pass the time, asked, "Hey, Umi, how long have Keith and I been in the Magic Mangroves, exactly?"

She looked upwards, as if trying to remember, and looked back at me, and very confidently said, "About 5 days, I'd say." My expression morphed from curiosity, to pure shock.

"Wait, then how come I haven't been hungry or tired, this entire time," I asked.

Umi apologized, "Oh, I guess I forgot to explain, sorry. Time doesn't exactly pass the same way it does on the outside world, where you're from. So, really, It's only been about a day. Or at least, on the outside world." I relaxed, despite being still confused. I guess it was just more comforting to know I might not be dying.

After what seemed to be hours of walking around the Metal Village, I finally asked Damien, "Hey, Damien, is it? Where exactly are we? I mean, the Metal Village doesn't exactly seem that big."

Damien froze, and turned to me, apologizing, "Guys, I'm so sorry. I don't know where we're going. The king ordered me to lead you guys to the other end of the village, and I can't refuse an order from the king, but he also never lets the guards leave the castle, and-" He started trailing off.

I put my hand on his armored shoulder, and reassured him, "Hey, it's okay. We'll just ask some other people for directions, and-"

"Oh, we can't do that," he interrupted. "The king's guards usually only talk to the civilians if they need to be taken to the king, and that's usually only if they're in huge trouble."

Umi pushed through Ber and Keith, and, with the most serious of looks, instructed, "Follow me." We followed.

Somehow, Umi knew exactly where to go, as she led us to the other side of the village. She really did know her way around the Magic Mangroves. I noticed that Damien started to get worried.

"Um, hey guys, maybe we should start hurrying," he suggested.

"Why, what's wrong," I asked.

Damien hesitated, "Well, it's just that-" In the middle of him talking, someone, who looked like they were in their teens, came from around the corner of a building, tackled Umi, and rounded another corner, running away with her. "I'm the guard of the Northern Metal Castle. The Northern and Southern ends of the Metal Village are at war. I was saying we should hurry before I'm recognized, and we start getting attacked. Now, let's go save your friend!" He pointed onward, and looked up, heroically.

"Umi," I corrected him.

"Yes, Umi! That's what I said! Let's go save Umi," he yelled, charging after the boy carrying Umi.

Ber, Dimma, Nick and I all chased after him. I heard Nick, behind me, mutter to Dimma that Damien annoys him. They then proceeded to argue about manners for the rest of the rescue.

When we turned the corner, the boy wasn't there, but there were two more turns. We all came to an agreement that Damien and Nick were the only two who could properly fight, or even stand a chance in a fight, so Damien went left, while Nick went right. I followed Damien, and Dimma, Ber and Keith followed Nick. I could still hear Dimma and Nick arguing.

Immediately upon rounding the corner, I could hear the sound of Umi struggling, and I looked forward to see the young man at a dead end, holding a knife to Umi's throat, holding her close, so she couldn't just escape.

"Stop, Northerners," the boy demanded. Damien and I froze accordingly.

"Young sir, I can promise you right here and now that you don't want to be doing this right now. I mean no harm to you, but if you continue I will not hesitate. Please release the woman," Damien demanded, in response.

"Okay. Okay, fine, I'll let her go," the boy began. Umi immediately looked relieved. "I'll let her go, if you go back to your pathetic king, and tell him to surrender his kingdom to the much superior king of the Southern End!" Damien drew his spear, and the boy laughed. "Lord, you Northerners really are pathetic. You're so helpless, you still believe that spear can save this woman, even from this distance!"

"Actually," Damien smirked, "the spear was a distraction." The boy's eyes widened for a moment, and then he lurched back and screamed in pain, dropping his weapon and releasing Umi. He collapsed forward onto the ground, revealing a dagger lodged in between his shoulder blades. "We should probably run now. Let's get the others and get out of here," Damien suggested. Umi and I agreed, Umi still shaken, and we followed Damien to where we came from, and Ber, Dimma, Nick, and Keith were waiting for us there. Damien didn't even stop, and instead just gestured for them to follow.

41

"So, what happened? I see you guys found Umi," Keith asked.

"Well I'm pretty sure Damien killed someone," I said, glaring at Damien. Keith wore a look of terror.

"Oh, relax, Metal spells disappear after a couple hours. He should be fine," Damien attempted to reassure us.

Keith corrected Damien, "Well, actually, the removal of the dagger would cause him to start dying faster, due to blood loss, and-"

"Hey, how did you-," I interrupted Keith, before he continued rambling on.

"How did I know I would have to use that spell? I didn't. A good fighter is always prepared," Damien boasted.

"Actually," I corrected him, annoyedly, "I was going to ask how you used a spell without saying its name. Or did you say it without me knowing, somehow?"

"Oh, it's simple, Hidden Blade is a Metal spell that summons a dagger which is telekinetically controlled by the user, and can only be seen by Metal Magic users, until it's lodged into someone's poor, clueless body," he explained.

After a short distance of running, we were at the other end of the Village. Obviously, we couldn't simply walk through the castle, as we would immediately be recognized, and most likely killed. As Damien, Keith, Umi, Nick and I contemplated what to do, I heard Dimma yell the words "Ice wall," with her hands held towards the sky, and, suddenly, a giant wall of ice appeared in front of her, in between her and the steel wall. Once the ice wall was up, Ber held her hands out towards the ground, and murmured the word "Thorny Vine," and vines, with rows of pointed thorns, began sprouting from the ground.

Ber then looked over at us, and yelled, "Hey Dame! Can I call you Dame? Do you have any spells that can turn things to metal?"

Damien, confusedly responded, "Um, yes to both questions. Why do you need to turn something to metal? And what do you need to turn to metal?"

"While you dumb-dumbs were talking about what you should do, me and Dimma over here actually figured out what to do. She made a wall of ice, because the holes in the steel wall will show, but the Ice Wall will disappear, and I made some vines, which we need to be metal, so it can break the ice easier, and we'll use the metal vines to climb the Ice Wall. So get your armored butt over here, and make these vines into metal," Ber demanded. Damien dropped his spear, and ran over to the two others.

"Metal coat," he said, holding his hands out to two vines, one to one vine, and the other to a different vine. Metal began spreading throughout the two vines' exteriors, starting from the bottom, up. He tapped one, to make sure the spell worked, and it rang, like a bell. It had worked. "Now," he continued, "I'm only making two of them metal for now, until you can prove this'll work."

Ber cracked her knuckles, plucking the metal vines out of the ground, and smirked, "Gladly." She planted one of the vines into the wall of ice, lifted herself up, and planted the other vine into the wall, higher than the first. She repeated this, effectively scaling the wall.

"Huh," Damien exclaimed, "I really did expect that to fail!"

Ber looked behind her, and scolded Damien, already halfway up the wall, "Of course it works! Me and Dimma are the smart ones here, haven't you realized? C'mon, keep up, Dame."

Keith nudged Damien, and mocked, "Yeah, keep up, Dame." Dimma began to scold Ber about how to talk to people, and to stop insulting their intelligence.

Ber had reached the top of the wall already, sat down, and yelled down, "What was that, Dimma? Sorry, I can't hear you from all the way up here. Maybe you guys should join me, so you can tell me what she's saying!"

Dimma stomped up to the wall, shoved two vines in Damien's face, which he used his Metal Coat on, and Dimma began her struggle up the wall. Either Ber is extremely athletic, or we all just weren't, as all of us struggled to scale the wall, except for Nick, while Ber did it seemingly effortlessly.

We had all finally made it up the wall, and we used the metal vines to bridge the gap between the two walls, so we could cross, and Dimma pointed at both ends of the vine bridge, and muttered, "Frost," and the two ends froze to their corresponding walls. I'm assuming she did this so the vines wouldn't roll away while we walked on them, and we all walked across, one by one. On the other side of the metal wall, the wall we were trying to cross in the first place, Dimma made two more Ice Walls, the first much smaller than the metal wall, and the second smaller than the first.

43

This effectively made steps for us. Since Damien was the one in a full suit of armor, he was the one who jumped down to the next wall, and caught us when we jumped down, so he could let us down gently. We repeated this order twice more, and we had reached the ground.

"Hey, we made it across," Damien exclaimed. "But where exactly are we?" Everyone looked around, clueless, trying to recognize where we were. The ground was magenta, shiny, and completely flat, aside for a few cracks here and there, and some large crystal structures protruding from the ground. There were dark purple crystalline trees in the distance, with thin, pink crystals for leaves.

Finally, Umi's eyes widened, and she said, "Actually, I've heard of this place before. I've never been here, thankfully, just heard of it.

Everyone, keep your guard up," she told us, "because we are now in the Mind Village."

Chapter Eleven

―――――⌇―――――

"Umi, what are you saying," I asked. "Why is the Mind Village so dangerous?"

"The Mind Village plays tricks on ... well ... your mind. Basically, anything can happen here, but only in your mind, and only you will see it. Anything you see here, could be being only seen by you, and you would never know. So I'm saying to keep your guards up, and not believe anything you see, because it might not actually be there," She explained.

We all nodded, showing that we understood, except for Ber, which is reasonable, she was a child, so we all agreed that someone should hold her hand at all times, so that she wouldn't get lost. Umi then showed us all the direction we needed to keep walking in, no matter what we see. Dimma volunteered to hold Ber's hand, and we were off on our journey.

We all started walking, and, foolishly, I touched one of the crystals protruding from the ground, and my head immediately began throbbing when I made contact, so I shut my eyes and held my head. When I opened them, the ground began shifting, and in the distance, the land was twisting, and changing colors. However, when I took a step, it was as if I was just taking a step onto regular ground, and the ground wasn't shifting at all. It was the crystals playing tricks on our minds. Of course, the first thing I decide to touch ends up being the things that cause illusions.

For what seemed like an hour, I tried navigating my way through a twisting and turning world, and finally, I gave up. I collapsed onto the ground, and cupped my hands around my face. I began to panic. I didn't know where I was, where I was supposed to go, or how to get there. I was hopeless. I couldn't call for help, either, because visions of my friends would appear and disappear at random intervals, and in random places, so I had no clue where they were.

"What are you doing here? I thought this was supposed to be a tourist-free space," a disembodied voice said. I looked behind me, and saw a man wearing nothing but baggy, magenta pants, hovering above the ground, with his legs crossed, and his hands in his lap. His eyes were closed, and he was very thin. One could tell that he hadn't eaten in a long time.

"Oh, well, I was actually trying to get out of here, and-," I said, wiping a tear from my eye. "Hey, how are you doing that? Actually, you know what? I've seen weirder here, what I'm more worried about is how you're not bothered by the hallucinogenic crystals."

"The crystals are created by Mind Magic users, to keep idiots like you out of here. They're supposed to make you start seeing things, and turn back, so we Mind Magic users can meditate, and focus our energy in peace, but obviously, since you're here, you didn't listen to the crystals' warning," he scolded.

"Well actually, I touched one of them, and couldn't tell which way was back," I explained.

The man opened his eyes, revealing light blue, shiny eyes, and asked, "You ... what? Why? Why would you touch anything here? Were you unaware that you get hallucinations from being here?"

"Well no, I was aware of the hallucinations," I explained. "I suppose my curiosity got the best of me."

He rubbed his forehead in frustration, "I knew you weren't a Mind Magic user, but I didn't realize that meant you would have absolutely no brain at all. Let me guess. You need someone who is unaffected by the crystals to guide you to where you want to go?" I silently nodded. I then told him that I needed to go to the more southern end of the Mind Village. "Fine. Let's go then." He dropped back down to the ground, as he straightened his legs, and, upon touching the ground, he wobbled on his feet, trying to regain his balance, but tried to make it seem like it was nothing, and walked off, with me following close behind.

It was very apparent that he wasn't lying, and he really wasn't affected by the crystals, as the walls I was seeing, he just walked through, as though they weren't there, and I hesitantly followed. The whole time, however, he would trip over his own feet every now and then. This made it apparent that he also didn't walk very often.

"Hey," I said, catching up to him, "you never told me your name. I mean, I'm pretty sure I would've died, had you not been there, and it would be nice to know my savior's name, so I know who to tell others about, right?" He rolled his eyes, looking away from me.

"You people are so sentimental. Saving one's life should not be considered saint-like, it should just be considered kind, and acknowledged no further. You may call me Etzel, for now," he rambled.

"I disagree strongly," I started, "as, the death of one person could strongly affect a wide variety of people, mostly in a negative way-"

He interrupted, "Please. Stop talking." Needless to say, it was a very quiet and upset walk.

We finally reached the opposite end of the Mind Village, where my friends were waiting for me, each with a disappointed look on their face, except for Ber, who ran up, hugging me, cheering that I'm okay.

"We all watched you touch the crystal, and immediately freak out, and stumble around, like an idiot," Umi said to me, unimpressed, with her arms crossed.

"It was honestly kind of sad," Dimma added.

Keith walked up to me, put his hand on my shoulder, and added, "Look. Buddy. We all love you. But you're an idiot."

Nick uncrossed his arms, and yelled, "Another new guy! Great! Fantastic! I'm out of here!" He turned around and walked away.

"You don't even know where you're going," Dimma yelled at him, annoyedly. He stopped, slowly turned back towards us, and walked hesitantly back to us. "So, who is this, anyway?"

I opened my mouth to tell them, and Etzel shushed me, saying, "You have no purpose in knowing my name, as you'll most likely never see me again. I brought you your troublesome friend, now, I will return to where I once was, and none of you will follow me, or even slightly bother me." He turned around, and began walking back.

"No, wait, we need you to come with us," I yelled.

Etzel laughed, "I don't mean to sound rude, although I don't care if I do, but why would I ever, even if you offered the world, do that?"

"Well, we're going to destroy the barrier here, so my friend and I can get out of here. You don't exactly seem like a likeable person, which makes me think you don't have any friends to talk to, so I can tell you that we need to break the barrier, because my friend and I don't use magic," I explained.

"You've interrupt my meditating," Etzel began, stompin towards me, "you argue with my perfect judgement, you force me to use my legs, and now you insult me? I will never, ever join you. Good day, sir." He turned around once more, and began walking off.

"Hm," Keith stepped up. "What a shame. I thought you'd be up to the challenge, Etzel. You seemed pretty strong, I thought you could be strong enough, mentally, seeing as you are a Mind Magic user. I guess you just aren't good at that, either. Come on, Joan, let's go, this coward isn't worth it."

Etzel froze, and clenched his fist, turning his head slowly. "Don't think I don't know what you're doing," Etzel grinned. "I understand completely the art of manipulation. I accept your 'challenge'. I will show you just how strong I can be, not falling for your trap, but to show you how small, and weak your mind is to mine." He walked slowly over to Keith. He put his face very close to Keith's, and glared at him, saying through gritted teeth, "You win. For now. You've succeeded, sure, but I will teach you to regret getting me to come with you." He walked past him, and continued walking, gesturing for us to follow. "Come, let's go destroy the barrier! As if that would work in a million years!" We followed.

CHAPTER TWELVE

W hen we exited the Mind Village, we were back to the sign that read "Magic Mangroves," in front of the swamp, with two stone paths leading away from it. I went back to when I knew nothing about either paths, amazed at how I ended up back here.

"Wait, how do we get out of here? There's a wall around the entire Magic Mangroves," I asked.

Umi walked up to the part of the wall directly parallel to the "Magic Mangroves" sign, and pulled the wall open, revealing that that specific part was made of vine. We all walked through, and she followed.

Keith looked at the shredded bits of boat that lay on the sand of the beach, and asked, "Okay, so, Joan, buddy, pal. Once we break the barrier, what exactly is our plan? Our boat is shattered, and even if we found a way to fix it, we've basically seen the entirety of the Magic Mangroves, and there was no sign of our boat driver." I looked down at my feet, and looked back up, opening my mouth to say something, but I couldn't think of anything to say, so I looked back down.

I looked back up, shrugged, and said, "Well, we'll figure it out." I walked off, to examine the shredded bits of boat, and to see if the barrier was even visible, which it was.

"He really is an idiot," I heard Etzel say behind me, and Keith agreed.

Within the couple yards away from the barrier, I could already feel my head begin throbbing. This barrier, I could tell, would be a problem.

I turned to face my group, and enthusiastically yelled, "Okay everyone, let's destroy this barrier!"

I somehow managed to organize all the magic users into a line, with Damien and Nick on the ends, and Ber in the middle, and everyone in between, from Ber to the two ends, went in order from shortest to tallest, on the shore.

"Ready," I asked. All of them nodded. "Fire!" On my command, all of them yelled a variety of spell names, with their hands outstretched to the barrier. With all of them yelling at once, I couldn't make sense of anything they said. Nick had electricity blasting from his body, Damien had metal spikes protrude from him, and shoot off at the barrier, there were vines coming from the sand below the water that was nearest to the barrier, whipping it, Dimma had freezing cold air pouring from her hands,

Umi was repeatedly hurling balls of flame, and Etzel had shockwaves coming from his head. After a few minutes of this chaos, all of them got tired and collapsed. Nothing happened to the barrier.

I let my hands hang in disappointment, and said, "What? Nothing happened! Not even a little rip! Not even a dent! How can this be possible?" I rubbed my chin, and began pacing back and forth. "Oh, I'm so sorry, are you guys okay?" I ran down to my magic-using friends, and tended to them, cancelling out the side effects of the overuse of their magic.

After about an hour of rest, Umi was the first to wake, and she asked, "Did we break the barrier?"

"No, I'm sorry," I told her. "I was surprised, though. I thought you said that it would take a combination of multiple different magics, right? We used six! How many could we possibly need?"

"Joan, I'm so sorry. I don't know, it should've worked, I honestly don't know what happened," she explained. "However, you could hopefully talk to Him, if he'll listen. The one with no name. He knows everything, he should explain."

"How do I get to him," I asked.

"He's at the center of the swamp, you have to cross the bridge, and he should be there. I've never been there myself, so please be careful," she instructed.

"Do you know whether or not he's dangerous," I attempted to reassure myself.

"Joan," she said, sarcastically, "do you really think an all-powerful, all-knowing man wouldn't be dangerous?"

I got up, and turned away, instructing her and Keith, "If anyone asks where I am, tell them I went to go talk to someone. Don't say who. Just say 'someone'. I don't want anyone worrying about me." I walked off.

I returned, once again, to the "Magic Mangroves" sign that I'd seen so many times before. Now, the bridge over the swamp, behind the sign, actually mattered to me. I began walking across. Despite it being a swamp, there didn't seem to be any bugs. Or fish, for that matter. It just seemed … empty. Devoid of life. All of the willow trees, by the swamp, were somehow grayed, but not rotting. The water was black, and murky. However, when I touched it, my hand did not come out black. It truly was just water. Strange, how even the water, which was never alive in the first place, even seemed dead here.

I walked across the bridge for what seemed like hours, and finally, I reached a small island, in the middle of the swamp. It was so far out from every edge of the swamp, that I couldn't see anything but water for miles. There was grass, the first time I'd seen grass since the Bio Village, but it wasn't right. It was gray, and overgrown. Every here and there, there would be a blackened flower, with a veiny texture on the stem. It was then that I saw a thin man, wearing ragged, ripped clothes, with wild black hair, bags under his eyes, and extremely pale skin, lying on the ground, not moving or breathing.

CHAPTER THIRTEEN

---❈---

"Um, sir," I called out, secretly hoping for no response. "Please," the man said, "leave me to die."

Confusedly, I asked, "What exactly are you doing?"

"Contemplating how my life became the constant torture and hell that it is now," he explained.

"And how exactly is your life constant torture and hell," I asked.

"What are you talking about," he asked. "I said nothing about torture. Or hell. Are you okay?"

"Yes you-," I began. I thought back to the moment in which I asked what he was doing, but in my memory, he hadn't answered at all, and just layed there. "You ... you didn't." I know now what he had done, but I would rather have my readers experience the story as I had, so I'll leave that for a later time. To this day, however, the memory remains in my head as him lying there, not responding, though I am positive that his response was actually what I wrote, hence, why I wrote it down.

"What do you want, kid," the man asked, annoyedly.

"Well, I wanted to know if you were Him. The one with no name," I asked him.

"Is that what they told you? The Magic Mangrove residents," he asked.

"Well, they said He should be here. The all-knowing, all-powerful-," I began.

"Yep," he said, standing up. "That's me. Why do you need me? What universe-altering mistake have you made, that you need me to fix?

Oh, and please don't call me 'Him', 'the one with no name', 'the all-powerful one', or anything of the sort, please."

"Oh, well, I ... I don't use magic," I began. "And neither does my friend. We wanted to break the barrier, so we can escape, and gathered a group of magic users, because a combination of multiple different magics would break it."

"Oh, that is what I told them, isn't it," he murmured.

"What you told them? What, exactly, do you mean," I asked.

"Look," he started, "I lied to the people of the Magic Mangroves. I am not all-knowing. I did not create this land. The barrier is not here to protect us from outsiders. Now, let me explain. Thousands of years ago, there was a boy, cursed at birth, with a type of magic that would possess him, take control of his body and mind, drain him of his sanity, his soul, his strength, simply because his mother was vain, and didn't like how the boy looked. Now, everyone has a birth magic, or, the type of magic they are naturally able to use. They just need to unlock it to figure out what it is, which can happen by just simply learning spells from the magic, or experiencing something that would activate it. Now, this boy was dejected from society, as, he had no moral compass, no sanity, no sense of 'right' or 'wrong', though he didn't know why. All he knew was that something was wrong with him. He grew to hate himself. He was homeless, too, due to his mother's cruelness, to top it all off. One day, he was attacked. This unlocked a rage in him, that he'd not known was in him. He hadn't known, at the time, that this was his doing, but the men who attacked him disappeared, in the middle of their attack, for seemingly no reason. Some time later, he realized this was his doing, and practiced this power. He learned to control it, and master it. He also learned that he could make other things out of the things he destroyed. With this god-like power, he got everything he wanted, through intimidation alone. He was eventually feared all throughout the world, as he also learned he could use any magic with this power, as long as he learned how to. One night, to get rid of him, powerful mages, from each magic, created an island, put him on the island while he slept, and sealed him there, using a barrier that not even Dark Magic, the magic he used, could break, for thousands of years to pass. Eventually, he was forgotten, and no one knew of him. Some time later, magic grew to be hated in the outside world, and magic users found this place, and populated it. Since they didn't know who this boy was, and therefore, didn't know of his power, the boy used this opportunity to make them believe he was a god, and that they should never cross him, in the hopes that, eventually, enough people would have faith in him to shatter the barrier, and let him free, to eventually find someone else who's birth magic is the same as his own, and pass this curse onto them, once he died, or immediately, if they were more powerful than himself. That boy, as you may have guessed by now, was me. So that's why I lied. I've been tortured by this curse all my life, and I just want to pass it on, so I may be freed. I need them to break the barrier for me. The curse also gives the victim age-immunity, in case you're wondering how I'm still alive. Oh, and I trust you to not tell anyone, because you now know that I can easily erase you from existence, so you'd have a deathwish to want to tell anyone. Do you understand?" I was about to nod, and he interrupted, "Don't answer that, I know you do. Any questions?"

"Well, yes, I do have one question," I answered. "Is that all you lied to them about?"

"I mean, those are the only significant ones," he told me. "The other lie I told was that people shouldn't come to me because I would be meditating, or something like that, but I only don't like people coming to me because I don't like talking to people. Other than that, I really can't remember any other lies I've told."

"Actually, I do have another question," I said, remembering why I came here in the first place. "How do my friend and I get out of here?"

"Oh, that, I don't know," he told me. "Why would I know that? If I knew that, I wouldn't be here right now, now would I?" I shook my head. "Now, please, leave me alone. I really don't like talking to people."

"Wait, please," I begged, "one more question. Just one more?"

"God, kid, do you not understand the concept of getting all your questions out at once," he asked. "Fine. One more question. But afterwards, I would suggest leaving. For your own sake."

"Could you," I hesitated. "Could you teach me my birth magic?" His eyes widened.

After a few moments, he burst into laughter, and exclaimed, "Kid, do you understand how long that would take? There are literally thousands of different magics! Yeah, it'll never happen. Have a nice day."

Axel Sainz

"But sir, please," I started.

"Hey, and don't call me sir," he demanded. "It's too formal. My name is ... wait ... what was my name again? It's been so long since I've had someone call me by it. You know what? Call me Cole. Sounds like the burnt remains of a beautifully deceptive fire. Just like me, being the leftovers of society! Now, please leave."

"Sir-," I began, but corrected myself. "Cole, if you could just allow me an hour to teach me what my birth magic is, I promise you won't regret it! I'll make it up to you, however I can!"

Cole rubbed his forehead, and said, "Fine. I know you're not going to leave me alone until I say yes, so I'll teach you. But only for an hour. That's it."

"Thank you so much, Cole," I exclaimed. "I promise you won't regret this!" I wasn't wrong. He would not regret it. But I definitely would.

After hours of strenuous training, and Cole losing track of time, enjoying my torture, he had given up. The skin on his arms and hands, I noticed, also started turning gray, and his veins were beginning to bulge.

"Welp," he said. "It's been fun, kiddo. But I have absolutely no clue what your birth magic could be." He looked down at his hands, and his eyes widened. This allowed me to see that his eyes also had a slight tint of red in them. "Oh, and would you look at the time! You should really leave now. Please." Then, I had an idea.

"You don't think my birth magic could be-," I began.

"No," he interrupted. "No it is not. And we're not trying it, either. Your endurance is much too low. Even if it was your birth magic, even I, the scum of the Earth, wouldn't do that to you. Now leave."

Offended, I yelled, "My endurance is not low! I can handle a lot-" He interrupted me by placing his right hand, which was completely black, with the veins of his right arm also completely black, on the front of my left shoulder, and muttered the word "pierce." His eyes, at this point, were completely red. Immediately, I felt an immense amount of pain in my shoulder, as if I had been stabbed. I clenched my shoulder, only letting go to lift up my collar to see if he had done any damage to me. There was a hole, barely half a centimeter in diameter. However, when I looked on the back of the same shoulder, there was another hole, identical in size, and exactly parallel to the one in front. I looked behind me, and there was an area of halved blades of grass. There were not too holes in my shoulder, the spell he casted had gone through my shoulder, and continued behind me. I clenched my shoulder once more, and let out a cry of pain. I looked back up at him, and he gave a me a cold look.

"Yes, your endurance is very low. Now," he continued, "since I like you, I would suggest you leave here, before the Dark Magic kills you. Oh, and don't worry about the piercing, it's only temporary. Just wanted to prove a point."

Shoulder still clenched, I walked away. I looked back, and he had turned away from me. He dropped down to his knees, and looked down at his hands. His neck was black by now, too. He completely collapsed, and I looked back and began running, afraid of what might happen, had I stayed.

CHAPTER FOURTEEN

I returned to the shore, where everyone still was. They had set up a campsite, with a campfire going, Dimma fishing with an actual fishing rod, in the water, and Ber also in the water, stabbing at any sign of movement she saw. Now was the first time since I had been on the island that I was able to visibly tell it was night, as it was pitch black, aside from the campfire, which lit quite a far distance. I could tell the campfire was made using Umi's Fire Magic, as it was much brighter than normal fire, and I could feel the heat from the couple yards away from it I was. Keith was the first to notice I was back, which only took a few moments. His face lit up, like a puppy, and he nudged Umi, who was sitting next to him, I assume against her will, knowing Keith, on the sand in front of the campfire, and she alerted everyone else. Nick and Damien were sitting behind Dimma and Ber, on the edge of the sand and water, with Damien attempting to talk to Nick, and Nick ignoring him. Etzel was across the campfire from Umi and Keith, meditating exactly how he was when I met him. Everyone ran to greet me, except for Etzel, who just looked at me, smiled, and continued meditating. Ber attempted to run out of the water to greet me, but fell, and Dimma ran back to carry her out of the water. Keith ran up to me and hugged me, with everyone else doing the same, except for Nick. Damien had taken off his suit of armor, revealing a tank top, and jeans, and he came over, hugging us all at once, cracking all of our backs. Well, besides Ber, who was too short to be affected by the spine-cracking hug of a loving giant. Damien backed up, releasing all of us, and everyone else backed up as well.

"So," Keith asked, "what happened?"

I struggled, for a moment, to try to figure out what to tell him without saying anything Cole told me not to say, and I decided to say, "We need more magic. If I can prove myself to him, he said he'd use his magic to help us." I said this with the intent of having them tell me a way to prove myself, so I can go back to him, and show him that I can handle whatever the Dark Magic is.

Nick snickered, "Well, that's going to be hard to do, what with the fact that you don't use magic."

"Well, I mean, you could help Ber and I catch fish," Dimma suggested. Ber vigorously nodded in agreement. I declined the offer, as I would have to do something completely alone.

Nick, walking away said, "Well, I don't know about you, but for me, building would be one of the best ways to prove yourself."

"You know, Nick," I said, "that may actually work!"

"Yeah, that's a great idea and all, but what exactly would you build? I mean, you're no architect, Joan," Umi asked.

I shrugged, and said, "Not sure yet, but I'll figure it out! I know I will!" Umi was right. I was no architect. I would have to build something simple. That, and I had little to no experience with gathering building materials.

Not knowing what I was doing, I stomped over to Cole's area. He was thankfully asleep. His arm was also back to normal, and there was a dip in the ground where he lay. I got to work gathering materials. I decided to build a staircase, since, or so I thought, they were fairly simply made. For an additional challenge, there were barely any building materials to use in Cole's area. And on top of that, none of the big stones I found were flat enough to build with. I looked for about a half hour more, and settled for the stones. I grabbed a smaller, sharper stone, and began carving away at the bigger stones I found, to make them flatter on the top and bottom, such that they are easy to build on top of. I spent hours finding large stones, carving them, climbing the steps, and placing them atop the tower. I had also given up trying to build a staircase, and instead, had begun building a step tower.

I had done this process, over and over again, for so long that, at a certain point, I could feel my head hurting, and looked up, seeing the air about ten feet above my head warping. I had almost reached the top of the barrier. The sun was up, by now. I was also able to see the entirety of the Magic Mangroves. "Has Cole taken advantage of this amazing view," I found myself wondering. It truly was an amazing view. I could see the ocean, the barrier, the horizon, everything. It was incredible. I sat down, and admired the view. I could even see the campsite my friends had set up. Dimma, Etzel, and Keith were the only three that were up, and Keith and Etzel were staring each other down. Etzel collapsed, holding his head. Keith began laughing, and he walked over to Etzel, who was also laughing, helping him up, and they began staring each other down again. It occured to me that Keith was using Mind Magic! Suiting, the two sarcastic, manipulative ones in our group are the two Mind Magic users. Had Keith been using Mind Magic all our lives, without either of us knowing, since we hadn't known about magic? Dimma, again, was fishing. It appeared that these seven had created an optimal team, from what I'd seen. The view had also been distracting me from the fact that my hands were bruised, scraped, and cut in several places, and I was starving.

"They're adorable," Cole said, levitating next to me. I jumped, startled. "They've really built a strong relationship with one another, haven't they?" I nodded. "So, what exactly was the point of this? Don't get me wrong, it's mighty impressive, it just seems pointless."

I stood up, and announced, triumphantly, "This step tower was meant to show you that my endurance isn't low, and I can handle the Dark Magic!"

"Kid, you're insane," he shook his head. "But, you have proven to me that you can handle it, so I might as well teach you." He snapped his fingers, and, suddenly, I was back on the ground, and he slowly drifted back down to the ground, shortly after. "Before we begin, you are aware that, if the Dark Magic likes you better than me, which will most likely happen, considering you are still sane, in-shape, and young, you will begin a downward descent into a constant state of madness, torture, and pain, correct?" I swallowed hard, and nodded. "Okay. I'm going to ask you to close your eyes, and become the most hateful, cruel version of yourself, for a moment. Think about anything and everything that makes you angry or hateful, and channel that energy." I did as he commanded, and closed my eyes. I imagined the anger I felt when Keith abandoned me. The fear I felt in the Ice Village. The pain of Umi's medicines on me, the frustration of

Damien killing the young man, the anger of Etzel and I arguing. When I opened my eyes, all I saw was red. "Now, quickly, look at that flower, focus on it - that part's important, don't get distracted, you could cause mass destruction - and say 'deconstruct'," he instructed, pointing at a wilted flower. I did as he instructed, and pink lines rose from the bottom of the flower, branching out to the other lines, creating sections. Then, each section of the flower separated, outwards from the center of the flower, and stopped, as if they were frozen in time. Lastly, they all fell in unison, each turning black as it fell, and disappearing before touching the ground. The flower was completely gone, with no trace. I looked at him for approval, and he gave me a thumbs-up. He stopped, and said, "Wait for it." Suddenly, the veins in my legs turned pitch black, spreading to the rest of my body, until it reached my head, then my entire body felt immense pain, worse than any I had felt, even in the Magic Mangroves, and I collapsed. The pain still haunts me today.

"What is happening to me," I screamed, desperate for anything, absolutely anything, to distract from the pain, grasping at my throat, squirming on the ground.

"It's trying to make you its host," he explained. "I warned you about this, didn't I?" He had. But he hadn't warned me of anything from this level. The rest of my legs began turning black, which spread much slower, and brought a much worse pain. I lifted up my shirt, and my torso was twisting, convulsing, pulsing. I tried screaming. I tried crying. I couldn't do anything. I looked up at Cole, and he just shrugged. My whole body felt like it was about to fall apart, and I could do nothing about it. The blackness reached my chest, and I was no longer able to breathe. I grasped at my throat, choking. I felt my chest tightening. I put my hand over my heart, and could feel no heartbeat. The blackness had almost reached my face, and it spread slower and slower as it continued. Then, suddenly, it receded, and I was able to breathe again. Everything went back to normal. I felt my body, and nothing was convulsing, or anything of the sort. Everything was back to normal. I looked back up at Cole.

He walked up to me, leaned over me, and asked, "So. What do you feel?"

"Pain," I groaned.

"No, other than that, obviously," he said, frustrated. "Like, do you feel, for example, emptiness? Sadness? Blankness?" I shook my head. "Dang it. I mean, oh, yay! It decided to keep me as its host! How exciting! It is strange that you suffocated for a moment, though. That never happened to me. And it took way longer to spread through you than it took for me. I guess you're just too weak. It had nothing to take over. Weird." I felt ashamed. However, I somehow also felt pride. I suppose it was because I, once again, had escaped the claws of death at my throat.

"So," I asked, "what ... what exactly happened to me? Will I be okay? And what exactly did you mean by 'if the Dark Magic likes me better'?"

Cole shrugged, "I don't know. You'll probably be okay. Oh, and, magic, in case you didn't know, is basically alive. It thrives when people use it, and the less people use it, the more powerful it will be, since it has less room to spread out to, and, usually, it has one person, usually the first person to use it, who is the 'host', and the magic is extra powerful for them, but they also have much worse side effects." He walked away, saying, "And hey, if you're not okay, you asked for it. You've done whatever happens to yourself." He lied back down in the spot he originally was.

I got up, brushed myself off, and took in the realization that I now had unimaginable power, and had opened a new chapter in my life.

Chapter Fifteen

———— ❧ ————

For the next couple of days, Cole trained me in the art of Dark Magic, teaching me how to be more precise in my aim with my deconstruct, teaching me to do it quicker, teaching me that he, because he's mastered the Dark Magic, doesn't need to utter the name of a spell to use it. He even taught me the spells "reconstruct," which allows me to construct anything of the same mass as anything I've deconstructed, and that I can even combine the masses of things I've deconstructed to reconstruct, and "copy," which allows me to instantly learn any spell I'm affected by. At nights, I would return to the campsite, and help my friends with whatever they were doing.

One day, however, I had returned to Cole's quarters, and he had his hands outstretched to the ground, with large chunks of it disappearing, one by one. "What are you doing," I asked, bewildered.

He looked at me with a mad joy, and responded, "I'm destroying this stupid island! I don't need it anymore! I have another Dark Magic user with me! Together, kid, we can break the barrier, and claim our rightful thrones, as kings of the pathetic outside world! Let's get revenge on the slimes that locked me in this hell!"

I yelled at him, "I'm no king, Cole. You're no king, either, seeing as this island was made with the only purpose of getting rid of you! People live here, Cole! Entire generations have grown up here! There are so many people who love this island, this island is home to so many people, you can't just destroy it!"

"Oh, can't I," he asked me, looking back down and continuing. "Join me already, kid! You know you want to be king. I know you want to be king. Everyone wants to be king, kid. You're no exception. Don't think you're so special, just because you believe in your so-called 'morals'." I stumbled back, and ran away. I could hear him yell from behind me, "You'll come around to it, I know you will!"

I returned to my friends, out of breath. Dimma and Ber weren't fishing, and Ber was dancing around with a fish, around three and a half feet long, which I assumed she caught, and Dimma and Umi were cheering her on. Keith and Etzel were talking, I'm not sure about what, and Damien was somehow making Nick wheeze with laughter. Everyone was getting along very nicely, and Umi noticed that I was clearly distressed, and walked over to me, asking what was wrong. I requested she gather everyone, so I could explain what had happened.

Ber and Dimma were still bouncing up and down with joy, Nick was giggling, and Keith and Etzel were joking around. I requested everyone silenced, so I may explain. I couldn't explain what I had saw, without explaining most things that had happened, which I was instructed to not talk about. Since I've never exactly been good at picking the most important details out of a story, so I had just explained everything.

Once everything was said and done, no one was smiling anymore, and had a look of distress or concern on their faces, instead. However, Keith, confusedly asked, "So, why didn't you just disassemble him, then and there?"

"Because, Keith," I explained, "I see him as a sort of friend, in a weird sort of way. We've spent so much time together, it feels like he's an old friend. I can't simply just end his life with a single word like that!"

Keith nodded, trying to understand my empathy. Etzel had a look of deep focus on his face. Keith put his arm around him, and asked, "What're you thinking, my guy?"

Etzel lit up, and exclaimed, "I have a plan!" He had proceeded to explain that they would surround Cole, without him realizing, and I would talk to him. If he hadn't stopped after a while of me trying to convince him, we would strike. We could hopefully draw out the Dark Magic, and escape, before we got harmed, and the Dark Magic, as it's been proven to do, would tire him out, and we would have enough time to figure out a way to permanently neutralize him. He also explained that the order they would be in would be Keith and Nick, two of the three people who used area-of-effect type magics, on either side of the bridge, Etzel on the other side of the small swamp-island, and Dimma and Umi would both be on the same side, either the right or left side, so they can cancel the side effects of each other's magics, and Ber on the opposite side of them with Damien to keep watch of her, surrounding Cole with area-of-effect magics, and aimable magics.

Keith laughed, and Etzel asked, "What? Is there something wrong with my plan?"

Keith, still laughing, responded, "No, no, that's not it at all. I'm actually laughing because it's perfect! Let's do it." Everyone nodded in agreement.

We practiced the formation, and our synchronization, all the way through the night, until morning. Then, everyone got into the swamp, and assumed their positions. I walked across the bridge, heart pounding. I saw Cole, who was still holding his hands out to the ground, but he wobbled on his feet. His eyes were half-shut, and the chunks of ground were disappearing at a much slower rate.

He looked up at me, smiled, and said, "I knew you'd come around. Come, join me." I walked up to him, and formed two chairs with my reconstruction, sitting down in one, motioning for him to sit down in the other.

He sat down in the chair opposite to me, and I explained, "So, I've thought about this whole thing, and, no, I still don't agree with you, but, I understand. You're excited to get off of the island." I could see rage building within him. "But there's no need to destroy so many people's home, Cole. So come with me, let's just live peacefully in the outside world, and-"

He stood up, and yelled at me, "No, you do not understand! You could never understand what it's like to go through what I've been through! If you truly understood, you'd side with me, and help me get revenge on the people who locked me in this hell that I've been tortured with!"

"Cole, calm down, revenge will get you nowhere good, all it could possibly lead to is war," I tried explaining.

"Well that's not my fault, now is it," Cole yelled. "Maybe my mother shouldn't have cursed me with this power, maybe people should be more considerate to those who can't control how they act, maybe, just maybe, those mages shouldn't have immediately resorted to locking me away, to rot for eternity. Now, if you'll excuse me, I will continue, and you will help me break the barrier when I finish." He once again extended his hands to the ground, and began destroying it. The hole was massive, at this point.

Etzel stood up, and looked at Cole, with his hand outstretched towards him. Cole grasped his head in pain, looked around wildly, spotted Eztel, and, with cold, red eyes, and a pitch black hand, outstretched his hand toward him. Pink lines began forming from the soles of Etzel's feet, to the top of his head his head, branching out to one another, just like the flower. Then, just like the flower had, Etzel fell apart. And, just as the flower bits had, each piece disappeared before it hit the ground. I, out of panic, ran over to where Etzel was, and collapsed on my knees, holding my head in my hands.

Then, I heard Keith scream, "You bastard!" He sprinted at full speed toward Cole, with a rage of which I'd never seen. Cole simply flicked his hand toward him and sent him flying. He hit the ground with a grunt, as Cole lifted himself into the air. With that, Damien, Bur, Dimma and Umi all uncovered themselves at once, and began casting spells at Cole. Without even looking at them, he deflected most of them flawlessly. One fireball hit him on his left shoulder, however, causing blackness to instantly spread from the point of impact, to the rest of his arm. Umi shot off another fireball, and Cole caught it with his blackened hand, and threw it back, with twice the speed, and the fireball grew in size.

Dimma jumped at Umi, pushing her out of the way, and the fireball hit the ground, causing an explosion, sending Dimma flying. Upon hitting the ground, Dimma almost instantly fell unconscious. Cole held his shoulder, as if restraining himself. Damien, in an attempt to protect Ber, began swimming away with her. Cole noticed this, and his blackened arm outstretched towards them. They both lifted out of the water, and were sent flying, Damien hitting a tree, stunned, and Ber sliding across the ground, immediately falling unconscious. Nick sent a wild bolt of electricity into the open, hitting Umi, Cole and I, stunning all three of us. In the moment of time he had, Damien came running at Cole, a flurry of hovering daggers following close behind. He skidded to a halt, and held his hands forward, sending all the daggers flying toward Cole. About five of them hit him, three in his torso, one grazing his throat, and one in his left arm, and the rest slowed down, and fell to the ground. Cole's entire body became black, including, for the first time, his head and whites of his eyes, with his pupils and irises turning blood red, and neon red, respectively. His head twitched, and he removed the blades from his body, with no hesitation, as if he were removing a article of clothing, and the wounds from them instantly healed, as he pulled them out.

He looked at Damien with a look which I can only describe as pity, and said, with a deep, demonic voice, "You shouldn't have done that." Damien looked up at him with fear, and stumbled back, trying to run away, and Cole outstretched his arm toward him, lifting him off the ground, beginning to disassemble him.

Without even realizing I was doing it, I heard myself saying, "Disassemble." The blackness immediately completely left Cole's body, as he realized what was happening.

He looked at me, with fear in his eyes, dropped to the ground, and begged, "Kid, you don't want to do this. Please, anything that happened was not me, it was the Dark Magic, please don't become like me. You're making a mistake, kid, I can promise you that right now. Please, we could be kings-" Just like that, Cole had fallen apart and disappeared, and was no more. Damien fell back to the ground, completely fine, and felt his body, checking to see if he was still alive, and, when he realized he was, he came running towards me, and hugged me, lifting me off the ground. He could tell I was still in shock about everything that had happened, and went to go tend to everyone who had been injured, which was everyone but Nick, who happily joined him.

CHAPTER SIXTEEN

T he next day, I didn't get to wake up, since I never slept in the first place, but Ber's wounds were treated, Dimma was put in a more comfortable position until she woke up, and Keith's and Damien's bruises were treated.

Keith walked over to me and asked, "So. Is Etzel ... gone?" He sounded like he was struggling to get the words out of his mouth.

I stood up, and responded, "Not if I have anything to say about it." I took in deep breaths, closing my eyes, and, imagining Etzel, muttered, "Reconstruct." This had been the first time I had attempted to bring something back, exactly as it had been before deconstruction, through reconstruction. A few moments passed. Nothing. I looked at Keith, and shook my head. He kneeled down, putting his head in his hand. I kneeled beside him, putting my arm around him. Damien came up behind him, and also put his arm around him. Ber ran up, and tackled him, however, she was not enough to knock him over, so she just ended up hanging from his neck.

The, I heard Etzel's voice say, "What's all this ... emotion ... is this ... empathy? Have I grown a valid relationship with you people? Do I ... care about you guys? Gross." Keith looked up at Etzel standing over his kneeling body. Etzel giggled, and everyone rushed towards him for a hug. Well, except, of course, Nick. However, even Nick was touched by this moment, clearly, as he even put an arm around Etzel, laughing that we're all crazy.

We had returned to the campsite, and Umi asked, "So, now that we have a Dark Magic user on our hands, and no other problems we have to solve, should we attempt to break the barrier again?" Everyone nodded, including Keith and I, now that we had something to contribute to the attempt at breakage. Everyone assumed the positions they were in, during the first attempt. Then, all at once, everyone began firing off spells at the barrier. However, this time, a small area of the barrier began to warp, like a piece of paper. I saw my opportunity, and cast deconstruct on the area that was warped. The pink lines spread from the point of weakness, instead of from the ground. They spread past what we could see, and, after a few moments, a loud popping noise, and the warping effect of the area behind the barrier disappears. I walked close to where the barrier was, and there was no effect. I looked behind me, and gave a thumbs-up. Everyone cheered.

I walked back to Keith, and asked, "Well, I guess it's time to figure out a way home, huh?"

Be piped up, and exclaimed, "Wait! Before you do that, I was actually wondering … can I … well … can I come with you guys? I don't exactly have anything here for me, anyways. No offense, Dimma."

"None taken," Dimma said, "I don't exactly have much here for me either. Would you mind if I came too?" After Dimma and Ber, everyone else began asking to come with, for different reasons, Damien to escape the kingdom and the war of the Northern and Southern ends of the Metal Village, Nick to escape his bad reputation, Umi to live a life in the outside world, and Etzel to learn more about the outside world.

"Well, I-," I attempted.

Keith interrupted, "Of course, all off you can come!"

I pulled Keith to the side, and scolded, "You do realize that if they come with, we would be responsible for finding them homes, right?" He nodded. "And how exactly do you expect to be able to do that, as two college students?"

"Look, don't even worry about it," he explained, "my parents bought a summer mansion thing, like, a year ago, remember? I'll just tell my mom that some friends are in a rough place, and need to use one. The ones who are left over can stay in our dorms. Honestly, Joan, big underestimation of my brain power."

We joined back with everyone else, who were conversing about how exciting life in the outside world would be, and Keith repeated, "So, you can all come with us!"

"Hey, an immediate upside to bringing us is that you don't need to figure out a way to get home, I can just freeze the upper layer of the ocean, leading to wherever you came from, and we can use that to get out of here," Dimma exclaimed

Etzel groaned, "Are you serious? I've never even been to the outside world, and even I know how long of a walk half of the Atlantic Ocean would be! And I just started using my legs again 3 days ago, in Magic Mangroves time, no less! That's only about a day in outside world time! Wait, is that right?" He looked at Umi, who was the only one who had been to the outside world, and she nodded. "Yes, a day in outside world time!"

Keith and I looked at eachother, and I looked around, saying, "Well, I'm pretty sure most of us can handle it, considering we've walked around most of the Magic Mangroves." Etzel stuttered, looking for a new complaint.

"Look, I'll go after Dimma, Keith, and Joan, and partially melt the layer, so it can be a fun water slide for you, you big baby," Umi explained.

Thanks to the warping effect of the barrier being gone, and Keith knowing the magic that raises every skill of your mind, it did not take very long at all to find where we came from. Well, that is, if you don't count about three hours as very much. Dimma agreed to be the one to run back and retrieve everyone else.

About an hour later, I could see Umi and Dimma, side-by-side, sliding, as Umi blasted flame at the ice ahead of them, making a slide. Ber followed close behind, riding on Damien's shield, like a sled. After that came Damien and Nick, Both on their stomachs, doing tricks, to outdo the other. Finally, behind everyone else, sliding around, trying to get up, and failing, over and over again.

After everyone had reached land, I asked a bystander walking by, "Excuse me, sir, do you mind telling us what state we're in?"

"Well, of course I would! Surprising that you wouldn't know by just looking around, you're in Florida, kid," the man responded. I shuddered, reminded of Cole, with the way he called me "kid." On the other hand, I was also very happy that we had somehow ended up in the place we needed to be, first.

We found our car, and began our drive back. This time, however, it was much easier, considering the fact that I had gotten used to not eating or sleeping.

I stopped at Keith's house first, to get a confirmation from his parents to use the summer "mansion," as Keith called it. His parents agrees, and I drove to the summer house, which was not far at all, and barely took about a half hour. I dropped everyone off, except for two people, who were Etzel and Ber. Ber immediately said she wanted to stay with me, and Etzel pretended to be "just fine" with staying with Keith, but even I could tell that he was ecstatic. Everyone said their heartfelt goodbyes, and we left. Don't worry, reader, it wouldn't be the last time Keith, Ber, Etzel and I would be seeing them. That's a story for another time, though.

We had reached our dorms, learned that it had only been about two and a half days in outside world time since we'd been gone, ate like animals, and everything went back to normal. At least, as normal as things could get as a Dark Magic user. Well, that's my story. I would like to thank you, the reader, for reading this story. I also want you to learn from this, that, exploring new things often leads to good outcomes. Mostly. That, too, however, is a story for another time. Go out and enjoy life, readers!

The End

About the Author

—⚬⚬⚬—

A xel's imagination was developed at a very young age. Although he does not consider himself a "true" writer, he does find inspiration in sharing his stories.

Made in the USA
Las Vegas, NV
14 December 2021

37709125R00049